Dear Parent:
Your child's love of reading starts here!

Every child learns to read in a different way and at his or her own speed. Some go back and forth between reading levels and read favorite books again and again. Others read through each level in order. You can help your young reader improve and become more confident by encouraging his or her own interests and abilities. From books your child reads with you to the first books he or she reads alone, there are I Can Read Books for every stage of reading:

SHARED READING
Basic language, word repetition, and whimsical illustrations, ideal for sharing with your emergent reader

BEGINNING READING
Short sentences, familiar words, and simple concepts for children eager to read on their own

READING WITH HELP
Engaging stories, longer sentences, and language play for developing readers

READING ALONE
Complex plots, challenging vocabulary, and high-interest topics for the independent reader

ADVANCED READING
Short paragraphs, chapters, and exciting themes for the perfect bridge to chapter books

I Can Read Books have introduced children to the joy of reading since 1957. Featuring award-winning authors and illustrators and a fabulous cast of beloved characters, I Can Read Books set the standard for beginning readers.

A lifetime of discovery begins with the magical words **"I Can Read!"**

Visit www.icanread.com for information
on enriching your child's reading experience.

I Can Read Book® is a trademark of HarperCollins Publishers.

Marley: Snow Dog Marley   Copyright © 2010 by John Grogan   All rights reserved. Manufactured in China. No part of this book may be used or reproduced in any manner whatsoever without written permission except in the case of brief quotations embodied in critical articles and reviews. For information address HarperCollins Children's Books, a division of HarperCollins Publishers, 10 East 53rd Street, New York, NY 10022.
www.icanread.com

Library of Congress Cataloging-in-Publication Data is available.
ISBN 978-0-06-185393-7 (trade bdg.)—ISBN 978-0-06-185392-0 (pbk.)

10   11   12   13   14   SCP   10 9 8 7 6 5 4 3 2 1   ❖   First Edition

I Can Read!

READING 2 WITH HELP

SNOW DOG

Marley

**BASED ON THE BESTSELLING
BOOKS BY JOHN GROGAN**

COVER ART BY RICHARD COWDREY

TEXT BY SUSAN HILL

INTERIOR ILLUSTRATIONS BY
LYDIA HALVERSON

HARPER

An Imprint of HarperCollinsPublishers

Winter had arrived.

Cassie, Baby Louie,

and their big puppy, Marley,

looked out the window.

Snow fell all around.

"Have you ever seen so much snow?"

Cassie asked Daddy.

Daddy smiled.

"Never quite this much," he said.

Marley ran to the door and barked.

"Marley wants to play in the snow!"

said Cassie.

Daddy grabbed a shovel.

"Okay, Marley," he said.

"But before we play,

we need to work."

Everyone put on coats, hats,

mittens, and scarves.

Then they went outside.

Daddy shoveled the walkway.

Marley shoveled, too.

Daddy was surprised.

"Thanks, Marley," said Daddy.

Cassie and Baby Louie

made a snowman.

"Don't eat the carrot nose,"

Cassie said to Marley.

12

Marley didn't eat the carrot.

Cassie was amazed.

"Good dog, Marley," said Cassie.

Mommy called the family in for lunch.
"Please get the snow
off your boots," she told them.
Marley waited while Mommy
dried his paws.

"Marley's being so good today,"
said Mommy.

"I wonder if it's really our dog
under all that fluff," she joked.

After lunch, it was time to take

soup to a sick friend.

Mommy poured some soup into a pot.

She left the rest of the soup

to cool.

Then everyone went outside,

and Mommy put the pot on the sled.

Daddy began to pull the rope.

Marley pulled, too.

"Marley's a snow dog!" said Cassie.

"He rescues people in the snow!"

Daddy let go of the rope.

Mommy frowned.

"Is it a good idea

to let Marley pull the sled?"

"You heard Cassie," said Daddy.

"Marley's a snow dog!"

Mommy smiled.

Everyone held hands

so that nobody would slip and fall.

Marley followed, pulling the sled.

Marley was doing a good job.

The soup pot was still standing,

and he hadn't spilled a drop.

Then Marley saw a kid

throw a snowball.

Catch that ball! thought Marley.

Marley started to run.

"Catch that soup!" yelled Mommy.

Marley dove through a snowdrift.

He lurched, he lunged, he leaped. . . .

25

Marley caught the snowball
in his teeth!

Daddy clapped wildly.

"Good catch!" said Daddy.

Mommy glared at Daddy.

"Bad snow dog," she said.

Cassie ran to the sled.

The pot was still on it.

"The soup is safe!" cried Cassie.

"Amazing!" said Daddy.

"Marley didn't spill a drop!"

The family delivered the soup.

Then they walked home.

Marley ran ahead.

"Marley is a snow dog, after all,"
said Mommy.

"But he's still our Marley!"

said Cassie.